Winnie

April Renner Curtsinger

Illustrated by B. Teresa Campbell

ISBN 978-1-0980-9740-0 (paperback)
ISBN 978-1-0980-9742-4 (hardcover)
ISBN 978-1-0980-9741-7 (digital)

Christian Faith Publishing, Inc.
832 Park Avenue
Meadville, PA 16335
www.christianfaithpublishing.com

Printed in the United States of America

To God, always my first thank you and praise. Without Him, I am nothing.

To dad, AKA "Papaw" from my first book, *Boone*. You earned your angel wings just before my second book's release. I dedicate this one to you. You were a constant in our lives, and I don't know what we'll ever do without you. I know you'll keep them laughing in heaven. Until we meet again, daddy, I love you.

Hey there! You may remember me from the book named after me—*Boone*. That's right, it's yours truly! If you haven't read it, I highly recommend it. It's the story of how my owner, April, saved me from life on the streets. Living with April and her son, Luke, has been amazing! I am now safe, healthy, and VERY well fed! We take walks every day, I have toys to play with, and most importantly, I am loved beyond measure.

1

Once April rescued me, things were going great. They had to leave most mornings for some place called work and school but would come back later in the afternoon. April came home during the day when she could to share her lunch with me. At first, I'd muster up my saddest puppy dog eyes hoping she wouldn't leave, but then she told me if she didn't go to work, there wouldn't be money to buy my food, so I figured I'd better let her go to this place called work!

I could tell it made her sad to leave me alone. She started mentioning adopting a brother or a sister for me. At first, I thought, *I don't want to share the love and attention I get! Things are fine the way they are!*

But then I got to thinking, it could be fun to have someone to play with. Someone like me to chase and fight over my toys with, he-he.

I had been with April about six months when, one day, she came home with a strange-looking box with holes in it. She said, "Boone, I have a surprise for you! Come meet your new sister! Her name is Winnie."

Nothing could have prepared me for what I saw next. She reached into the box and pulled out the strangest looking dog I had ever seen! It had this long skinny tail, pointy little ears, stiff hairs sticking out around its mouth, and was all splotchy with different colors. And it definitely did NOT smell like me! When I got up close to it for a sniff, it hissed at me and swatted me with these sharp long claws! I jumped back and gave April a look out of the corner of my eye as if to say, "No thanks, you may return this impostor to the store!"

4

April patted my head and said, "It's okay, Boone, she'll just need to get used to you. Cats sometimes take a little longer to warm up to you. She's just a kitten, so you will need to be gentle with her. We're a family, and everyone is different in their own special way, but we love each other despite those differences and can learn a lot from one another. God tells us to love everyone, not only those who are just like us."

Well, all I heard was "CAT." Are you kidding me? A CAT! No way, no how, lady!

Okay, Okay, stuff it, fuzz ball! Winnie interrupted. This is MY story! You've had the chance to tell your story. This book is titled, *Winnie*, is it not? I will take over from here.

Hi, guys, I'm Winnie. Yes, Winnie, the cat, not Winnie, the dog.

It all started when I was taken from my mom, along with my brothers and sisters, to some place called the shelter. It was loud and smelled funny. The people there split us up into these small cages. There was no room to run and play. The workers were nice and tried to keep us comfortable. I knew they were doing the best they could for us.

People would come in and take the other cats sometimes. I heard the workers say they were going home. They made it sound like "home" was a good place and were happy and excited for them. Every day I wondered if I would get to go to this place called home, but the people would walk right past me.

Then one day, there she was. As soon as she walked in the door, she spotted me, and I didn't take my eyes off her. I knew she was picking me. I was finally going "home" like the others had.

When we got to April's house, I met my clumsy goofball brother, Boone. My human brother, Luke, asked April how she knew I was the right one. April said she had prayed for God to guide her decision in picking the right pet for their family. She said that no matter how big or how small the decision is, we should always ask for God's guidance and God's will to be done. She said she knew as soon as she saw me that I was the one. So even though I wasn't crazy about this Boone character, I knew that God didn't make mistakes, and this was somehow going to work out just the way it was supposed to.

At first, Boone scared me. He kept pouncing on me and barking loudly. April had a safe place for me, a big room all to myself where Boone couldn't get to me. I could come out when I wanted, but I liked staying in there with my bed and toys. Boone would sit there ALL day and watch me through the glass door.

One day, I was a little bored with playing all by myself. I tiptoed out of my room very quietly, but I accidentally stepped on a squeaky toy. Boone came running and chased me all around the house! I started to have fun when I saw he just wanted to play with me and wasn't going to eat me! I even started hiding from him and pouncing on him when he walked by. I still like doing that!

Yeah, yeah, yeah, and we lived happily ever after, Boone interrupted, jokingly. I got used to your funny looks and weird smell and thought maybe I could be your friend after all. I remember when you got sick and wouldn't play. You laid in your bed sneezing and wouldn't eat. April was worried. You'd only been with us a week or so.

She took you somewhere in the car one day, and I didn't know if you were coming back. I suddenly felt an ache in my chest. I hoped you were okay. I hoped you would be coming back home to play with me again. April came back with you later that day and said you had been to the vet. You had an infection that was common with shelter animals. You had medicine to take and were going to be okay. I was so relieved! That's when I knew I loved you. But you still look weird, Boone added, playfully.

Not as weird as you! Winnie laughed as she lovingly patted Boone on the head. But seriously, it's a good life. Boone and I play together and then snuggle together on the couch. April comes home and snuggles us both. I realize now that we're all just as God made us, special in our own way. We are called to love one another, whatever size or color, whether furry or bald. I love my little family and wouldn't want it any other way!

The real Boone and Winnie

About the Author

April Renner Curtsinger grew up in Mount Vernon, Kentucky, a small rural town where people wave when they pass you on the street and everyone knows your name. She attended Eastern Kentucky University and received a degree in child development. She has a love for children's books and animals, mainly the ones with fur. She combined the two, with their simple, lighthearted innocence. April now lives in Elizabethtown, Kentucky, where she enjoys spending time with both her human family and the furry ones alike.

CPSIA information can be obtained
at www.ICGtesting.com
Printed in the USA
LVHW071130090821
694898LV00002B/2